Encyclopedia Brown

and the Case of the
Carnival Crime

Encyclopedia Brown

and the Case
of the
Carnival Crime

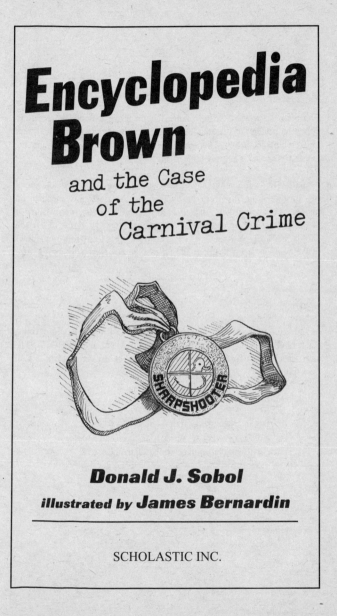

Donald J. Sobol

illustrated by **James Bernardin**

SCHOLASTIC INC.

ISBN 978-0-545-49557-8

12 11 10 9 8 7   15 16 17/0

Printed in the U.S.A.   40

First Scholastic printing, September 2012

Designed by Jason Henry

For Richard Siegelman,
my Number One Fan among school teachers

———————

CONTENTS

Encyclopedia Brown

and the Case of the
Carnival Crime

The Case of the Vanished Sculpture

The town of Idaville had a secret.

From the outside Idaville looked like many seaside towns its size. It had several banks, three movie theaters, and two delicatessens. It had churches, synagogues, and clean beaches.

Nevertheless, Idaville was different. No one, grown-up or child, got away with breaking the law in Idaville.

Police across the country puzzled over how Idaville did it. Whose masterful mind cracked the hardest crimes? The popular choice was Chief Brown of the Idaville police force.

The Chief was brave and smart. He always knew what to do with an especially hard mystery. He went home to eat.

His only child, ten-year-old Encyclopedia, solved the case at the dinner table. Usually he needed to ask only one question.

Chief Brown wanted to tell the world about Encyclopedia. Yet who would believe him? Who would believe a fifth-grader belonged in the Detective Hall of Fame?

So Chief Brown said nothing and neither did Mrs. Brown.

Encyclopedia wasn't looking for the spotlight. He had read more books than almost anyone and never forgot what he read. That was how he had gotten his nickname. Only his parents and his teachers called him by his real name, Leroy.

Thursday night the Browns were having roast chicken and mashed potatoes for dinner. As his father poured gravy on his potatoes, Mrs. Brown said, "Careful, dear, you don't want to drown them."

Chief Brown put down the gravy boat. "Sorry," he said. "This museum case has me stumped."

"What happened?" asked Encyclopedia.

"A small sculpture was stolen yesterday from the Idaville Museum. It was a statue of the Roman god Mercury."

"How small is small?" asked Mrs. Brown.

"It was about a foot tall," said Chief Brown. "And pretty heavy, too, because it was carved out of marble. The robbery took place a couple of hours after the museum had closed."

"Doesn't the museum have security cameras and an alarm system?" asked Mrs. Brown.

"They certainly do," said the Chief, "and

they're good ones. We reviewed the tapes. They show that all the museum visitors left when they were supposed to."

"After that?" asked Mrs. Brown.

"After that," Chief Brown said, "the security camera was mysteriously turned off. Now, it made sense that the alarm system was not activated for the night since people were still at work inside. But the security cameras are never turned off on purpose. That points to an inside job. The problem is, there were three employees inside the museum at the time the robbery occurred. One was the Curator of Antiquities, the second was a security guard, and the third was a janitor. They all claim to be innocent."

"The Curator of Antiquities would certainly know how much a statue like that was worth," said Encyclopedia.

"He ought to," his father said. "In fact, he was the one who told us the statue is worth a hundred thousand dollars. However, he's not familiar with how to turn the security cameras on and off."

"The security guard could do that," said Encyclopedia.

"He could," agreed his father, "but he claims he was nowhere near the control room —which is where the switch off happened. We dusted for fingerprints. The place was clean as a whistle."

"What about the janitor?" asked Mrs. Brown.

The Chief shrugged. "He says he knows nothing about art. If you need advice on washing a floor, though, he's your man."

"Have you arrested anyone?" questioned Mrs. Brown.

"No," said the Chief. "The problem is, the three suspects alibi one another. They were all in the building at the same time. The security guard was making his nightly rounds when he saw the curator working late in his office. They even said hello to each other. The security guard also saw the janitor washing the floor of the lobby. Both the security guard and the curator saw the janitor later rolling the pail away with the mop over his shoulder when the floor was done. They waved to him, too. Apparently, the staff doesn't stand much on ceremony. They're pretty friendly."

"I don't suppose you can arrest them all?" asked Mrs. Brown.

"No," said the Chief, "not unless we thought they were working together. We don't think that. We've interviewed the other museum employees, and these three don't seem to have known one another especially well. We've checked their work schedules. Nothing out of the ordinary. And that's too bad. I'm afraid if we don't zero in on one of them soon, the trail will go cold."

"Don't worry about that," said Encyclo-pedia. "I believe I know who's artfully hid-ing his guilt."

WHO DOES ENCYCLOPEDIA THINK IS THE THIEF?

(Turn to page 77 for the solution to "The Case of the Vanished Sculpture.")

The Case of the
Glittering Diamonds

During the year Encyclopedia helped his father solve crimes. When school let out for the summer, he helped the children of the neighborhood as well. He opened a detective office in the family garage. Every morning after breakfast he posted his business sign outside the garage. He kept his fee to only twenty-five cents.

Encyclopedia Brown was sitting in his agency reading the business section of the newspaper. There was an article on the stock market quoting some financial experts. Half of them thought the market would go up. The other half thought it would go down. There was also an item about an Idaville man who had started a company that made triangular-shaped cardboard boxes. Encyclopedia was wondering what kind of company he might start for himself when he heard a voice in front of him.

"Buy low, sell high, and never be afraid to leave some of the profit for someone else."

These words of wisdom were uttered by Dollar Bill Pesada. He was in the sixth grade. Everyone called him Dollar Bill because he was careful with his money. He always had his eye out for good investments.

Encyclopedia put down the newspaper. "That's sound advice."

Dollar Bill smiled. "The trick is knowing when the right moment has come." He took out a quarter and put it down on the empty gasoline can. "I won't waste your time with small talk because time is money."

"Good to know," said Encyclopedia.

Bill went on. "I'm here for a reason. I want to hire you to check out a new opportunity I've just heard about. Bugs Meany is selling shares in a diamond mine."

"Bugs Meany?" Encyclopedia groaned. "Ugh."

Bugs was the leader of a gang of boys called the Tigers. They were so underhanded that sometimes they had trouble raising their arms over their heads.

"This could be a great opportunity," said Dollar Bill. "If what he's claiming is true, I could double or triple my investment in no time."

"If I know Bugs," said Encyclopedia, "he'll be the only one making money on this."

"In that case," said Dollar Bill, "we'd better investigate at once."

They found Bugs standing in front of the Tigers' clubhouse, an unused toolshed behind Mr. Sweeney's Auto Body Shop. A crowd of kids had gathered around him. Bugs was talking about the diamond mine Dollar Bill had mentioned.

"You know how women wear diamond engagement rings?" said Bugs.

The crowd of kids sounded off to let him know they did.

"Some of the diamonds found in this mine are too big and heavy to put on a finger. You'd barely be able to lift one with two hands."

"Is that all diamonds are good for?" asked a kid in the front.

Bugs said, "No, no, they're used in machines and other things. Believe me, it won't be hard to find a home for any diamonds dug out of this mine."

The kid in front still wasn't satisfied. "I'm not so sure. What if your cousin just made the whole thing up?"

Encyclopedia feared Bugs might take a swing at the kid for saying something like that, but Bugs surprised him.

"I don't blame you for doubting," Bugs said calmly. "After all, nobody wants to be tricked into losing money."

The kids laughed a bit uneasily.

Bugs grinned. "My cousin knows that, too. He didn't want you to take my word for anything. That's why he sent me some proof."

Bugs drew a box out of his pocket and opened it.

Everyone moved forward for a closer look.

"Oooh!"

"Wow!"

"Just look at the size of that diamond!"

"That's right," said Bugs. "It's nearly as big as a golf ball. Look how it glitters in the sun. You don't see diamonds like that every day. It's probably worth thousands. My cousin didn't mind sending it to me because it's one of the smaller ones."

"If diamonds like that are the small ones, why do they need us?" the first kid asked.

"I'll tell you," Bugs said grandly. "The way my cousin explained it, the diamonds don't come out of the mine all polished and everything. They're dark and rough. Getting them ready to sell costs money. The miners aren't a big group. They don't want to sell out to some huge company. That's why they're looking for small investors to chip in."

"Makes sense to me," said Spike, a Tiger, who was watching from the side. "It's one of those rags-to-riches success stories. Luckily, it sounds like there's still time for us to get in on the big money."

Dollar Bill pushed forward for a closer look. "Can I hold the diamond?" he asked.

Bugs snapped the box shut. "I'm surprised at you, Dollar Bill. You're known as someone who recognizes the value of a good investment. I just told you this diamond is probably worth thousands. If I let you hold it, you'd promise to be careful. But then everyone else is going to want to hold it, too. What if one of you slipped and dropped it or just scratched it while passing it around? The diamond could be ruined."

"Sorry, Bugs," Dollar Bill apologized. "I don't know what I was thinking." He turned to Encyclopedia. "It seems like Bugs has thought of everything. This is the time to act fast."

"You mean run as fast as you can," Encyclopedia said. "That diamond is a fake."

HOW DOES ENCYCLOPEDIA KNOW?

(Turn to page 78 for the solution to "The Case of the Glittering Diamonds.")

The Case of the
Tempting Toys

Encyclopedia always looked forward to the annual Idaville Fair. The town made a point of dressing up for the event. Doors were freshly painted, and red, white, and blue bunting hung from every window on Main Street. But none of those things, nice as they were, explained why Encyclopedia looked forward to the fair itself.

There was no mystery involved. The explanation for Encyclopedia's enthusiasm could be summed up in one word—pie. The fair was famous for homemade pies of every variety—apple, peach, cherry, lemon meringue—Encyclopedia liked them all. His stomach had convinced him that Idaville had more fine pie makers per square mile than anywhere else in the state.

As Encyclopedia walked home after getting a haircut, preparations for the fair were in full swing. There was a lot of hustle and bustle. The fair put everyone in a good mood. One high school girl seemed to be an exception. She was setting up one of the concession stands. As Encyclopedia passed by, she kicked a table leg.

"Ouch!" she muttered.

"Are you all right?" Encyclopedia asked.

"Yes, yes," she said. "Or I would be if I didn't go around kicking table legs."

"Then maybe you should stop," said Encyclopedia.

"Good idea. I'm just feeling upset." She took another look at him. "Hey, you're Encyclopedia Brown, the boy detective."

Encyclopedia admitted it.

"My little sister, Carrie, talks about you a lot. I'm Mindy Harmon." They shook hands. "You've arrived in the nick of time."

"I have?"

"If you're as smart as Carrie says you are, I've got a case for you," Mindy said. "You charge a quarter, right?" Without waiting for an answer, she fished a quarter out of her pocket and handed it to him. "That makes it official."

"Tell me what happened," said Encyclopedia.

Mindy's dog, who was sitting nearby, barked twice.

"Quiet, Cooper!" said Mindy. She turned back to Encyclopedia. "Don't mind him. He always barks at strangers. It doesn't seem to scare them much."

"Something was stolen?" asked Encyclopedia.

Mindy nodded. "A large box of stuffed

animals is missing from my supplies. They were meant to be prizes for some of the games. It's too late now to get new ones."

Encyclopedia was a little relieved that no pies were involved. "When did you notice the animals were gone?"

"I had been carrying stuff from my car. I was depending on Cooper to keep an eye on things."

She looked down at her dog. "Didn't do a very good job, did you?"

Cooper just wagged his tail.

"The toys didn't wander off by themselves," said Encyclopedia. "How long ago did this happen?"

"I'd say about an hour ago."

"Did you see anyone come by?" asked Encyclopedia.

"No. I would remember because I could have used some help setting up."

"Did you see anything suspicious at all?"

Encyclopedia asked. "Maybe just someone hanging around."

Mindy snorted. "I wouldn't call it suspicious exactly, but I did notice Biff Bumpkin watching me work from a distance."

"You know Biff?" Encyclopedia asked.

"We've never met," Mindy said, "but I've seen him around school. He doesn't have the best reputation."

"Did he watch you for a while?" Encyclopedia asked.

"He seemed to. Then I went to my car again for another box—and when I got back the stuffed animals were gone."

"What about Biff?"

Mindy stopped to think. "He was gone, too, and he hasn't come back."

"Biff lives around the corner," said Encyclopedia. "Let's go see if he's home."

"All right," Mindy said. "I'm not relying on Cooper this time. I'll get one of

Encyclopedia, Mindy, and Cooper found Biff sitting
on his porch.

the other volunteers to keep an eye on my booth."

Encyclopedia, Mindy, and Cooper found Biff sitting on his porch. He smiled unconvincingly at the sight of them.

"Hey," said Biff, "it's the Answer Man. Or maybe I should say Answer Boy. Give me a minute and maybe I can think up a real stumper for you."

"While you're thinking, you can answer a couple of our questions," Encyclopedia said. "Mindy here is missing some toys that belonged to the fair. She saw you nearby and wondered if you saw anything."

"What kind of toys?" Biff asked.

"Stuffed animals," said Mindy. "They're supposed to be prizes."

Biff laughed. "Do I look like someone who collects stuffed animals? Wait, Answer Boy, don't answer that yourself. I'll do it for you. No, I do not."

"So you don't know anything about it?" said Encyclopedia.

"Nope. You're barking up the wrong tree. I like the real thing. Come here, boy," Biff said, motioning to Cooper.

Cooper came forward and Biff patted him on the head. "Any other questions?"

"You know," said Encyclopedia, "Cooper was there the whole time. He saw exactly what happened."

Biff shook his head. "Too bad dogs can't talk," Biff said. "If they could, I'll bet you'd get right to the bottom of your little mystery. The way things stand, you're out of luck."

"Maybe not," said Encyclopedia. "Luck has nothing to do with it."

WHY DOES ENCYCLOPEDIA SAY THIS?

(Turn to page 79 for the solution to "The Case of the Tempting Toys.")

The Case of the Missing Songs

Chief Brown, Mrs. Brown, and Encyclopedia were waiting in line for Fiona Slocum's concert. Slocum was the chief's favorite country western singer.

"I can't believe Fiona Slocum is actually performing here in Idaville," he remarked. "I've heard her on the radio often. I never expected to see her performing live. You two will love her."

"We're lucky she's playing in Idaville," said Mrs. Brown. "She used to tour in big cities all over the world."

"I remember," said Encyclopedia. "Her first album, *Sweet Tea and Sour Grapes*, was very successful."

"That's right," Chief Brown said. "And she had that smash single, 'You're Over the Hill, Not Under It'—which was a tribute to her grandfather. That was two years ago. New acts have come along since then. She took some time off after the last tour. Something about recharging her batteries. Now she's back. Playing in smaller places like Idaville is a way to start the climb back to the top."

"Maybe you'll be able to get her autograph," said Mrs. Brown.

Chief Brown said, "Our seats won't get us close enough for that."

"You're the Chief of Police," Mrs. Brown reminded him. "Maybe something will come up that demands your attention."

"I doubt it," said the Chief. "Fiona's fans

are hardly a rowdy bunch. We're not expecting any trouble."

"Trouble may be on its way," said Encyclopedia. "Here come two of your officers."

Encyclopedia was right. The officers explained that the Chief was needed at once.

They led the Browns backstage. All kinds of people were wandering about making preparations for the concert. Among them was a tall man with a thick mustache that curled up at the ends.

"Why, you're Colonel Abner Singleton," said Chief Brown. "Fiona Slocum's manager."

"Indeed I am. And you, sir, are?"

Chief Brown introduced himself and his family.

"A pleasure," said the colonel. "My title is honorary. I cherish it, nonetheless. I only regret that we meet at such a difficult time."

"Why is it difficult?" the Chief asked.

"As I was telling your good officers, there's been a robbery."

"Of what?" asked the Chief. "Money? Jewels? Furs?"

"No, what's been taken are Fiona's latest songs," the colonel answered. "She was planning to perform them tonight for the first time. She had shown them to no one, not even me, and she had only one written copy."

"That would make the copy about as valuable as rare jewels," the Chief commented.

"I see you are a fan, sir," the colonel went on. He lowered his voice. "You may know that Fiona has gone through a bit of a dry spell lately. This concert tour was going to renew her career."

"Where were the songs taken from and when?" asked the Chief.

"From her dressing room, perhaps an

hour ago. At least that's when she first noticed they were missing."

"Where is Miss Slocum now?"

"She has asked to be alone."

"Can she rewrite the songs from memory?" Encyclopedia asked.

The colonel paced back and forth. "Perhaps another singer might. You see, it was
Fiona's gift to pour her heart and soul onto
paper. But her memory has never been
strong. Even when performing songs she's
done a hundred times before, she always
reads from the sheet music. I begged her to
entrust me with a copy for safekeeping. She
refused. She kept the new songs a secret."

"Are there any other facts for us to start
with?" asked the Chief.

"There is a suspect," said the colonel.

"Who would that be?" asked Chief
Brown.

"A fan who is crazy about her," the colo-

nel said. "Naturally, Fiona enjoys and appre-
ciates everyone who likes her music. This
one fellow, however, follows her around
from concert to concert."

"Has he done anything illegal in the
past?"

"Not that I know of," the colonel replied.
"Still, I'm sure he is guilty."

"Do you know his name?" the Chief
asked.

"His first name is Chuck. At least that's
the name he uses when sending Fiona his
fan letters."

The colonel rubbed his hands together.
"You've got to solve this case before Fiona
is scheduled to sing tonight. Without those
new love songs, her comeback will be ruined."

"If the fan is guilty, we'll find the proof,"
the Chief assured him.

"It's not the proof I'm worried about,"

said the colonel. "It's the songs that matter."

"I'm sure they're perfectly safe," said Encyclopedia.

WHY WERE THEY SAFE?

(Turn to page 80 for the solution to "The Case of the

Missing Songs.")

The Case of the
Home-run Hitter

It was a slow morning at the Brown Detective Agency. Encyclopedia and his junior partner, Sally Kimball, were playing catch in the side yard. Sally was working on her curveball till a customer arrived.

"If I'm going to win games this summer," said Sally, "I need to have more than one pitch."

"Are you sure?" said Encyclopedia. "Nobody seems to have much luck against your fastball."

"True," Sally admitted. "But if the batters wise up to the fact that that's all I have got, sooner or later they'll be pounding out hits."

"I'd say later," said Chip Caswell, riding up on his bike. "When it happens, I'll try to get a few balls to add to my collection."

Nobody liked to collect baseball souvenirs more than Chip Caswell. He saved the ticket stubs from every game he'd ever been to. His baseball cards filled six shoe boxes. He might have had even more if his parents hadn't complained that his hobby was taking over his room. He had collected signed balls, bats, cards, and caps from teams all over the country.

"Did you hear the news?" he asked.

"Does it have something to do with baseball?" asked Encyclopedia.

"I'll say. There's a new sports museum opening up in Idaville, and they've offered a spot in the main hall for a kid to donate something," Chip said.

"And you're ready to give?" asked Encyclopedia.

"Sure. If they pick something of yours, you get to have your name on a plaque for everyone to see."

"That's pretty exciting," said Sally. "But why do you need us?"

"The museum has put out a notice saying they will be examining donations at noon today. I figure there will be a long line of kids with stuff to donate. I want you to see what they have, and then tell me which of these I need to offer to make sure my donation gets picked," Chip said.

Encyclopedia looked at his watch. "It's eleven thirty now. I guess we'd better get going."

When they arrived at the museum, they got a surprise. There was no long line of

THE CASE OF THE HOME-RUN HITTER

kids. Only one person was standing there—
Sammy Jackson. He was one of Bugs Meany's
Tigers. They were so slippery, the truth
wouldn't stick to them if you pasted it on
with a bucket of glue.

"Where's the line?" asked Chip.

Sammy smiled at him. "You're looking
at it."

Chip shook his head. "I can't believe nobody else came."

"Oh, they came," said Sammy, "and then
they left."

"Why would they do that?" Encyclopedia asked.

"Couldn't take the competition," Sammy
explained. "Once they saw what I was offering, they just disappeared."

"And what have you got?" Chip asked.

Sammy smiled. He took out a box and
removed the lid. A baseball was sitting inside on a velvet base. "That, my friend, is

"Couldn't take the competition," Sammy explained. "Once they saw what I was offering, they just disappeared."

a baseball hit by the great George Herman Ruth. I'm talking about the Bambino, the Sultan of Swat, the greatest hitter who ever lived. Now, if this were simply a ball that the Babe had hit—even for an out—it would be valuable. This is more than that. This is a ball Ruth hit for a home run."

Chip gasped.

"Since you brought along Encyclopedia Brown," said Sammy, "I'm sure he will agree that Babe Ruth hit seven hundred and four-teen home runs over his long career. Isn't that right, Encyclopedia?"

"Yes," Encyclopedia agreed.

"I thought so." Sammy grinned at him. "By the way, the Babe ate even more hot dogs during his career than he hit homers. He was famous for downing as many as a dozen before some games. Those hot dogs are long gone. This baseball is not. In fact, it has a further claim to fame. This baseball was one that Babe Ruth hit on a day when he hit three home runs."

Chip had closed his eyes, as if trying to imagine the scene.

"The homer was hit in Yankee Stadium, home of the Yankees before the stadium was torn down," Sammy said. "I was never in Yankee Stadium. My great-uncle lived nearby and went to as many games there as he could afford. He never left before a game was over, and so he found himself sitting almost alone in the bleachers when Babe Ruth came up in the bottom of the ninth. The game itself was not in doubt. The Yankees were leading by three runs. My uncle liked to get his money's worth. This was his lucky day because when Babe Ruth took a mighty swing with two strikes, the ball sailed in his direction. It landed a couple of rows beneath him and bounced up to his waiting hands. The home run was not a game winner since the Yankees were already ahead, but it still represents a piece of baseball history."

Chip sighed. "What a story!" he said

Sammy nodded. "Not long ago my great-uncle passed away. He left me the ball in his will. I am not the baseball fan he was, and it seems only proper that the ball end up in a museum where everyone can enjoy it."

Chip turned to leave. "We might as well go, Encyclopedia. My collection is pretty good, but I don't have anything to compete with that."

"Don't be in such a hurry," said Encyclopedia. "I think we have a foul play here. That ball is a fake."

WHAT REVEALED IT AS A FAKE?

(Turn to page 81 for the solution to "The Case of the Home-run Hitter.")

The Case of the
Lazy Lion

From his seat in the big circus tent, Encyclopedia Brown had a good view of the acts in the center ring.

"I think these are our best seats yet," said Chief Brown.

"They're certainly the closest," said Mrs. Brown.

Every year, the Browns drove into town to see the circus. The owner, Phineas Dailey, was an old friend of the Chief's, and he never failed to send them tickets. The Browns, in turn, were always delighted to attend. The circus wasn't about tricks, the Chief liked to say. It was about skill, daring, and showmanship.

Encyclopedia agreed. He marveled at the motorcycle bikers who were riding inside a giant metal sphere without crashing into each other. He held his breath watching the trapeze artists somersaulting through the air. His lips felt hot when the fire swallowers closed their lips to cut off the air to the flames.

Only the lion tamer seemed a little bit off today. He could not get his lion, Felix the Ferocious, to do much of anything. He snapped his whip; he shouted into his megaphone—nothing seemed to help. The lion just lay there, casually flipping his tail from side to side.

The crowd tittered. The ringmaster came out with a wheelbarrow filled with steaks that he pushed to the lion tamer's side. The lion tamer threw several steaks to the lion, who didn't seem to notice. The whole audience was laughing now. The ringmaster shrugged broadly. Then he ushered the lion and the lion tamer out of the spotlight and hurriedly brought in a troupe of performing seals.

When the show was over, Phineas Dailey came in search of the Browns.

"An excellent show as usual," Chief Brown told him.

"We thoroughly enjoyed it," Mrs. Brown added.

"Especially the lion act," said Encyclopedia. "It was very funny. I didn't expect that at all."

"You weren't the only one," Mr. Dailey replied.

Now that the crowd was filing out, the Browns could hear shouting behind one of the curtains.

Mr. Dailey looked at the Chief. "I wonder if you could do me a favor and investigate the constant quarreling between our ringmaster and our lion tamer. Nothing official, of course. If you could spare a few minutes . . ."

"Lead the way," said Chief Brown.

The Browns followed Mr. Dailey backstage. It wasn't hard to find the lion tamer and the ringmaster. They were still yelling at each other in a corner.

The lion tamer was red in the face. "It's an outrage. It's sabotage."

"Nonsense," snapped the ringmaster. "Don't try to cover up your mistakes by playing innocent."

"Mistakes?" sputtered the lion tamer. "You're speaking to Majesto, the greatest lion tamer of our time. Perhaps of any time. Even the greatest, though, cannot work miracles with a drugged lion."

The ringmaster snorted. "Drugged, hah! A lazy lion is more likely. Lazy because of your poor training."

"Hold on a second," said Mr. Dailey. "Gentlemen, this is Chief Brown of Idaville and his family. The Chief's a personal friend who happened to attend today's performance. I've asked him to look into your, ah, disagreement."

"There's not much to look into," said Majesto. "I've been dating Lola, the trapeze artist. Her old boyfriend, Cocoa the clown, isn't very pleased about it. He must have drugged the lion sometime before the show started."

"Assuming you're right, when would he have had to do that?" asked Chief Brown.

"I would guess an hour before showtime."

"Not possible," the ringmaster stated. "Cocoa and the other clowns were practicing a new routine all morning, right up until the show started."

Majesto frowned. "Then someone else is responsible. I have made a lot of enemies on my rise to the top."

"Anyone in particular and nearby?" asked Chief Brown.

Majesto nodded. "It could have been Lola's brother, Bruno."

"He's the circus strongman," Mr. Dailey explained.

"Bruno's never liked me," the lion tamer said.

"You just can't admit to your own mistakes," said the ringmaster. "Inventing suspects doesn't change the facts." He turned to Mr. Dailey. "This act is really unacceptable, sir. I tried to cover up with that wheelbarrow of steaks."

"Which I knew nothing about!" Majesto protested.

The ringmaster sneered. "Luckily for you the audience didn't notice. If people think the show has mistakes, they'll want their money back."

Mr. Dailey turned to Chief Brown. "You see what I'm dealing with. We have to solve this mystery as soon as possible. Can you help?"

"What will help," said the ringmaster, "is firing the lion tamer. This kind of behavior cannot go unpunished. What if the lion returns to being a dangerous animal because of poor training? What if it happens in the middle of a performance?"

"That's ridiculous," said Majesto. "Felix would never do that."

"Just like Felix would never be lazy," retorted the ringmaster.

"You wouldn't dare say that if Felix were standing here!" said Majesto.

"Why not?" said the ringmaster. "Should

I be afraid he would eat me? After all, he did turn down the steaks."

"Hold on," said Chief Brown. "We probably should talk to Bruno and then we'll see."

The ringmaster snorted. "It's a waste of time. We all know who's guilty."

"Maybe not," says Encyclopedia. "After all, at the circus not everything is as it appears to be."

WHO DOES ENCYCLOPEDIA SUSPECT?

(Turn to page 82 for the solution to "The Case of the Lazy Lion.")

The Case of the
Explorer's Map

Encyclopedia Brown opened his agency door one morning to find ten-year-old Sarah Jenkins sitting outside. "Wow!" he said. "You're here early."

"I wanted to make sure I was first in line," Sarah said.

Encyclopedia looked both ways. There was nobody else in sight. "No problem there," he said.

"Good," said Sarah. "I need your help right away." She took out a quarter and placed it carefully on the old gasoline can. "You may not know this, Encyclopedia, but we've started a new club this summer. We're calling it the Lost and Found Club.

"The club members are all interested in explorers. The Explorers Club seemed like a boring name. Since explorers often get lost, and usually get found, we settled on the Lost and Found Club.

"Anyway," she went on, "we're very interested in old maps. If you look at an explorer's route on a map today, it doesn't look so amazing because we now know where everything is. In the old days, explorers had no idea what was waiting for them beyond the horizon. They had to be brave and skillful."

"And careful, too," said Encyclopedia. "A lot of them died before achieving their goals."

"Exactly," said Sarah. "So you can understand how excited we were when Nate

Switcher got in touch with us. He thought we would be interested in buying a map drawn by a Spanish mapmaker who accompanied Columbus on his historic voyage of fourteen ninety-two. Imagine what that trip must have been like. Sailing into uncharted waters . . . worrying about falling off the edge of the earth. . . ."

"Columbus wasn't concerned about that," Encyclopedia said. "Knowledgeable sailors knew the earth wasn't flat."

"That's a fact. I can picture it in my head. I see their faces peering into the mists," Sarah said.

"They had to deal with more than mists," Encyclopedia declared. "Certainly they had plenty of real things to worry about. Running out of food or fresh water. Fierce storms. Attacks from sea monsters . . ."

"Sea monsters?" said Sarah.

"That's the picture in *my* head," Encyclopedia said.

Sarah laughed. "We figured you could help, you being a detective and all."

"I can try," Encyclopedia said. "I think I've seen Nate around town. He's a high school senior, isn't he? Where would he get a map like that?"

"He says he found it at a flea market on a trip his family took to Spain. I checked on that," Sarah said. "The Switchers did go to Europe last summer. Since he bought it with his own money, his parents say he can do whatever he wants with it."

"Why is he singling you out?"

"I guess he figures the Lost and Found Club has the most interest." Sarah smiled. "And we do. He wants me to come over to his house for a look. I figured it would be good to get your opinion."

"Okay," said Encyclopedia. "Let's go."

When Nate saw them coming, he smiled broadly. "Glad you could make it, Sarah. Obviously, you know a good opportunity when you hear one. I see you brought a friend. How nice."

"So where's the map?" Sarah asked excitedly.

Nate laughed. "I understand your excitement. Imagine how I felt coming across the map under a pile of dusty papers. I have it right here." He took it out of a box carefully and laid it out on a small table.

"Behold!" he cried. "Columbus and his New World."

The map was yellow and stained. It was brown at the edges.

"Hmmm," said Sarah. "There isn't much on it. Just a few islands and the words 'Atlantic Ocean' printed in fancy letters."

"That's what makes it authentic," Nate said. "You have to remember that Columbus did not go too far north or south on his first voyage, so naturally the map doesn't show much of North or South America. Any map

"Behold!" he cried. *"Columbus and his New World."*

that showed all that might look truthful, but it would be a fake."

"True enough," said Encyclopedia.

"Exactly," Nate said smoothly. "Your friend knows what he's talking about. Don't forget that the word *'America'* itself did not show up on a map until fifteen hundred and seven, and it had nothing to do with Columbus. A German mapmaker named America after another explorer, Amerigo Vespucci. He didn't really do that much for the honor, but the name stuck."

"Nate seems to have his facts straight," said Sarah.

"He's on a roll," Encyclopedia allowed.

"As I said on the phone," Nate went on, "I could sell this map to a museum if all I cared about was the money. The way I figure it, museums have way too much stuff already. They can't even display most of what they own. I don't want this map to be hidden in some dusty vault. I want it to be bought by people who will enjoy it openly—like the Lost and Found Club."

"This map would be a real inspiration for us," Sarah admitted. "What do you think, Encyclopedia?"

"Keep your money in your pocket," the detective said. "That map will only take you in the wrong direction."

WHAT MAKES ENCYCLOPEDIA THINK THAT?

(Turn to page 83 for the solution to "The Case of the Explorer's Map.")

The Case of the
Arrowhead Hunters

Encyclopedia Brown and his friend Henry Millsap were sitting by a snapping fire deep in the woods of the Idaville Campgrounds.

"I can't believe I found three Indian arrowheads," said Henry.

He looked at them in his hand. The arrowheads were gray pieces of slate. Each one was about two inches long and had a chipped texture that looked like the scales of a fish.

"You deserve them," said Encyclopedia. "You searched long and hard yesterday."

"I have the mosquito bites to show for it,"

Henry remarked. He rolled up his sleeves to inspect the bumps.

The two boys had come to the campground with their fathers as part of an annual Idaville Father and Son camping trip. After setting up their tents, Encyclopedia and his father had gone fishing. Mr. Millsap had wanted to join them, but Henry had insisted on hunting for arrowheads. His father had kept him company. That meant mostly sitting on a log while Henry dug around in the dirt.

It had rained during the night and was still drizzling. Henry was in too good a mood to mind.

"As soon as we finish eating, I'm going to go out looking for more arrowheads," he said. "Want to come?"

This time Encyclopedia left the fish safe for another day. "Sure," he said. "Maybe I'll get lucky, too."

Henry stopped at his tent to put the arrowheads away. He was afraid to lose them by carrying them around. They went out and returned an hour later. It had continued raining, and they were both thoroughly wet.

"We didn't find another arrowhead," Henry mumbled glumly.

"We did find plenty of mud," said Encyclopedia.

"And bugs," Henry reminded him. "There was no shortage of bugs." He looked down at his clothes. "We brought a lot back with us. The mud, I mean, not the bugs. I'm going to change."

He ducked into his tent.

A few moments later he came out.

"My arrowheads are gone! Someone went through all my stuff."

"I don't suppose they left any clues," said Encyclopedia.

Henry frowned. "If they did, I probably destroyed them looking through everything."

"I'll go tell my dad," said Encyclopedia.

Chief Brown promptly questioned the other fathers, most of whom had been with their sons during the time the arrowheads had been taken. If fact, only three boys at the campground did not have any alibis. That was because their fathers had spent the morning sleeping in their tents.

The first was Frank Donner, who was cooking a hot dog over a bright fire.

"Sure I heard the kid shouting about missing arrowheads," he said. "You'd have to have been deaf not to hear him. This morning I was gathering wood for my fire here." He pointed at a pile of dry wood. "There's the wood—and here's the fire."

It was burning brightly in front of him.

Mr. Donner, who was already eating a hot dog, spoke up. "Listen to him, Chief. He's making good sense."

The second camper was Jack Muir. He, too, claimed to have been gathering wood for the smoky fire he was tending.

"I never heard of Millsap or his arrow-heads," he said, poking at the embers to keep his fire alive.

Mr. Muir kept shaking his head in dis-belief. "This is a terrible business," he said. "Just terrible."

The third camper, Teddy Rose, also de-nied having anything to do with the theft. "I wouldn't know an arrowhead if I fell over it," he said.

"Wouldn't know it," his father repeated.

"That's right, Dad." Teddy shivered. "If I had known it was going to rain, I would have stayed home where it's warm and dry. Out here it's not easy keeping this fire from going out." He coughed twice as the wind shifted and the smoke from the fire blew into his face.

All three boys let the Chief search through their packs to see what he might find. No arrowheads turned up.

"That doesn't prove much," Chief Brown observed. "Any of them could have the arrowheads hidden away somewhere safe. They could come back for them in a few days."

"It's hopeless," said Henry. "I mean, I want the arrowheads back, but I don't want to accuse an innocent person by mistake."

"Don't fret," said Encyclopedia. "I didn't want to speak up too soon in case the arrowheads were found in the search. I think now we can turn up the heat on the one who's guilty."

WHAT DOES ENCYCLOPEDIA MEAN
BY THAT?

(Turn to page 84 for the solution to "The Case of the Arrowhead Hunters.")

The Case of the
Courageous Camper

When Paige Dutton first walked into the Brown Detective Agency, she didn't stop right away. She just kept walking. She probably would have bumped into a wall if Encyclopedia hadn't spoken up. "Watch out!"

Paige stopped. "Oops," she said, putting down the book she had been reading.

Paige Dutton was a great reader. She probably had read almost as many books as Encyclopedia, but she only liked to read stories. So when it came to information, she knew Encyclopedia had her beat.

"I need your help," she said, taking out a quarter.

"Book trouble?" asked Encyclopedia.

"Not trouble, exactly," Paige said. "Buster Wilde has a cousin who just survived an incredible wilderness adventure. He and Buster think that the adventure would make a best-selling book. But they don't want to share the profits with some publisher. They want to make and market the book themselves."

"Sounds ambitious," said Encyclopedia.

"It is," Paige said. "Printing books costs money, so they're looking for investors. I've saved up a bit from babysitting, and I'd love to enter the world of publishing. This could be just the beginning. Someday I could have my own line of books."

"Have you heard the story yet?" Encyclopedia asked.

"No, Buster's going to tell it a little later today. I want you to hear what he says to see if the story rings true."

Buster Wilde was waiting for the kids behind the Idaville Public Library. About fifteen had gathered before Paige and Encyclopedia got there. Like Paige, most of them were serious readers who spent a lot of time at the library.

"I'm glad so many of you have come here," said Buster. "Today you will witness the beginning of a new chapter in publishing. Not everybody gets the chance to be part of something like this at such a young age. All of you are true pioneers."

"Tell us about the story," one kid piped up.

"Can't wait, eh?" said Buster. "All right, let's get started. As you know, the hero of the story is my cousin, Roger. Danger is his middle name—at least it should be after what happened to him.

"Roger was on a trip with his parents out west," Buster began. "They were in one of the national parks, the kind where the trees grow so thick you sometimes look up and can't see the sky."

Buster hitched up his pants and went on.

"Roger and his dad went out on a hike, and a sudden storm came up out of nowhere. The rain came pouring down, and the wind blew so hard they had trouble hearing each other. It was dark, too, because the storm clouds blotted out the sun. They got separated in the darkness. Now, it was bad enough that Roger was lost in a storm in the middle of the woods. Things suddenly got worse. The storm had awakened a hungry bear. When the lightning flashed, Roger saw the bear. Unfortunately, the bear saw Roger. Bears can run faster than people. You can't climb a tree to get away from them. Bears climb trees better than people. Roger knew both of these things. He ran for his life. The bear chased him. Roger would have been a goner for sure—except he came to the edge of a cliff."

"How did that help?" asked Paige.

"The wind had died down a bit, so Roger could hear water rushing below," Buster said. "He figured there was a river at the bottom of that cliff. Since his choice was to be eaten by a bear or to jump blindly into the river— he jumped."

Everyone gasped.

"The water was bitter cold," Buster continued. "It felt like needles pricking his skin. The good news was the bear didn't jump. Roger was safe. All he had to worry about now were the rapids up ahead. The current yanked him underwater. He struggled to the surface. Although pulled down again, he never gave up. Finally, he was washed ashore. For a long time he just lay there, shivering."

The kids who were listening shivered, too.

"Roger managed at last to get up," Buster told them. "The churning water had emptied all the supplies in his pockets except his compass. It was night now. Roger was afraid to sit still until morning, fearing he would freeze to death. He tapped the compass a few times. The needle seemed to be working. He knew the ranger station was near a lake to the east. He let the needle settle in that direction and followed it all night.

"The path was not easy. It seemed as if every root and rock had been carefully placed for him to trip over in the dark. He developed blisters on both feet and painfully hobbled along.

"When dawn came the next morning, he arrived at the ranger station. It was the best sunrise Roger had ever seen.

"So who wants in?" Buster questioned.

"I'm so excited," Paige whispered to

"I'm so excited," Paige whispered to Encyclopedia.

Encyclopedia. "This story has everything. What a way to break into publishing!"

"It's no way at all," the boy detective said grimly. "It's definitely time to close the book on this investment."

WHAT MAKES ENCYCLOPEDIA SO SURE?

(Turn to page 85 for the solution to "The Case of the Courageous Camper.")

The Case of the Carnival Crime

Every summer the carnival came to Idaville, filling the empty fields behind the high school with amusement rides and games. Over a long weekend, much of the town turned out to have fun and eat cotton candy.

On Saturday afternoon, Encyclopedia and his junior partner, Sally Kimball, closed the office in the detective agency early and went over together to check out the attractions. Sally liked the Ferris wheel, which at the top gave a fine view of the town. However, Encyclopedia didn't like riding it. Even though he understood all about centrifugal force, he didn't like spinning.

"You're sure you don't want to try the revolving teacups?" asked Sally.

"Better for me if I don't," said Encyclopedia. "Probably better for the teacups, too."

"Not fair!" cried Dexter Mumford, coming up beside them. He was a seventh-grader and small for his age.

"It's not really a question of fairness," said Encyclopedia. "My head—and my stomach—would say it was more a matter of common sense."

"Not fair at all," Dexter went on.

"I don't think he's talking about your motion sickness, Encyclopedia," said Sally.

"I feel sick, all right," said Dexter. "Sick about what happened to me."

"Why don't you tell us about it?" said Sally. "We're detectives. Maybe we can help."

Dexter stared at them. "You don't look much like detectives."

"We're in disguise," Encyclopedia said with a laugh.

Dexter slowly nodded his head. "Okay," he said. "I came to the carnival today to play the games. I do that every year. I've never won anything before. I figured maybe I was due."

"The science of probability doesn't really work like that," Encyclopedia explained.

Dexter blinked at him. "Anyway, I tried one of the shooting games with a rifle, hitting these little ducks that swim back and forth. You know the ones?"

"Yes," Sally answered.

"Okay," said Dexter. "I don't know why,

but for once I couldn't miss. The ducks went one way—I knocked them down. They went the other way—I knocked them down. I just had the right feel. When my time was up, I had the high score and won a sharpshooting medal."

"Great!" said Encyclopedia.

"Congratulations!" said Sally.

"Thanks," Dexter said. "Naturally, I was pretty excited. As I said, I'd never won anything before. A few kids came over to see what the medal looked like up close. I was happy to show them. Then they all left, all except one, another kid from my class, Max Bungleson."

Max Bungleson was one of the Tigers. They were so mean that milk would go sour if they looked at it the wrong way.

"He said a few nice things about my steady hands," said Dexter. "Then he asked me if he could hold the medal for a minute. I didn't have a good reason to say no, so I gave it to him. He held it for a few seconds. Then he put it in his pocket. When I protested, he just laughed. He said he deserved the medal for all the years he could have been picking on me and hadn't."

"Only a Tiger would think that made sense," Sally said. She turned to Encyclopedia. "We should help Dexter get his medal back."

"You can do that?" asked Dexter.

"If we can get Max to admit he took it," said Encyclopedia.

"You make it sound easy," Dexter said.

"That remains to be seen," Encyclopedia replied.

They found Max near the roller coaster, showing off the medal to a group of young admirers.

"I won this for my eagle eye," Max bragged. "Robin Hood had nothing on me."

"I'm sure he didn't," said Encyclopedia. "After all, he used a bow and arrow."

"That was his loss," said Max.

"It wasn't really his fault," Encyclopedia pointed out. "Guns hadn't been invented yet."

"Never mind all that," said Dexter, jumping in. "That medal's mine. I won it fair and square and you swiped it."

"I think you're a little confused," said Max, grinning broadly. "I don't blame you for wanting it. Medals like this are hard to win."

"Which is exactly what I did," said Dexter.

Max turned to the others. "As I was saying, I won this shooting those little ducks. They didn't know what hit them. Me and my six-shooters were on fire."

Dexter sighed. "I guess there's nothing we can do, Encyclopedia."

"Don't give up," said Encyclopedia. "We're not out of ammunition quite yet."

WHY NOT?

(Turn to page 86 for the solution to "The Case of the Carnival Crime.")

Solution to *The Case of the Vanished Sculpture*

Encyclopedia thought it was odd that the janitor would carry a wet mop over his shoulder after cleaning the floor. Surely the mop would leave drip marks. The only reason to carry the mop was because it wouldn't fit in the pail. And the only reason for that was if something else was in the pail besides the dirty water—something like the missing sculpture. Confronted with this information, the janitor confessed to the crime and returned the stolen sculpture. He's now cleaning floors at his new address—the state prison.

Solution to *The Case of the Glittering Diamonds*

As Encyclopedia knows, diamonds are the hardest substance in nature. Therefore, if the diamond Bugs had in the box was real, there was no reason for him to be worried about it getting scratched. Since he was worried, the diamond was clearly a fake. When faced with this fact, Bugs admitted that he made up the story so that the Tigers could afford to buy the supplies to make their own baseball diamond.

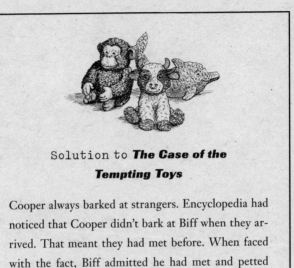

Solution to *The Case of the Tempting Toys*

Cooper always barked at strangers. Encyclopedia had noticed that Cooper didn't bark at Biff when they arrived. That meant they had met before. When faced with the fact, Biff admitted he had met and petted Cooper earlier when he was taking the toys. He had planned to impress some girls by giving them prizes he could have claimed to have won at the fair. Without the stuffed animals, Biff could only impress the girls with his charm—which meant he was really out of luck.

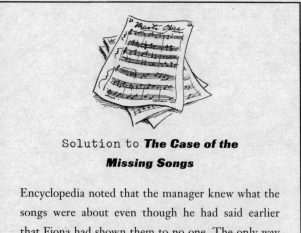

Solution to *The Case of the Missing Songs*

Encyclopedia noted that the manager knew what the songs were about even though he had said earlier that Fiona had shown them to no one. The only way the manager could have known they were love songs was if he had taken them himself. It turned out that Fiona was planning to fire him. He planned to "discover" the songs later, earning her gratitude and thereby continuing on as her manager. As things turned out, he was fired even sooner than he expected.

Solution to *The Case of the Home-run Hitter*

Encyclopedia knew that Babe Ruth of the Yankees had hit three home runs in a game four times. However, Ruth could never have hit the home runs Sammy described. The home team doesn't come to bat in the bottom of the ninth inning if it is already ahead, and Sammy had stated the game had taken place in Yankee Stadium, the Yankees home field. So the Babe could never have hit the home runs as Sammy said. Caught in his lie, Sammy confessed. He had found the ball in the back of his closet, but he figured if he was the only one left in the line when the museum opened, they would put his ball on display. When Chip took out some of the mementos he had brought, Sammy knew he had struck out.

Solution to *The Case of the Lazy Lion*

Encyclopedia had been surprised that the lion's sleepiness had been unexpected. After all, the ringmaster had brought out the wheelbarrow filled with steaks during the act—and it had to have taken time to prepare that. Therefore someone had to have known the lion would be unable to perform.

That someone was the ringmaster. He was hoping to make the lion tamer look bad so that he would have to leave the circus. That would improve the ringmaster's chances of dating Lola. Since he didn't want the performance to be ruined, he had prepared the steaks in advance. Once he was exposed, he confessed his misdeeds and was forced to clean up after all the animals for a month.

Solution to *The Case of the Explorer's Map*

A lot of what Nate said about Columbus and his explorations was true. Any first map of Columbus's might not have much on it. However, Columbus sailed under the Spanish flag for Ferdinand and Isabella of Spain. Anything written on the map, such as "Atlantic Ocean," would have been in Spanish, not in English. When Encyclopedia pointed this out, Nate quickly rolled up his map and sailed back home as fast as possible.

Solution to *The Case of the Arrowhead Hunters*

Encyclopedia noted that while all three campers had similar alibis, two of them, Jack Muir and Teddy Rose, were sitting by smoky fires. That indicated that the wood they were using was wet—which made sense because it was raining when they gathered it. However, Frank Donner's fire was burning brightly, which meant his wood was dry. That only was possible if he had gotten his wood before it rained and put it in his tent. Then he stole the arrowheads while the others were gathering their wood. When told this fact, Frank admitted he had taken the arrowheads, and he returned them and added three more that he had found.

Solution to *The Case of the Courageous Camper*

The story of Buster's cousin was certainly exciting, and it sounded possible until Buster explained that his cousin had turned his compass until it pointed east. Encyclopedia knew that compasses always point north toward the magnetic North Pole. Once Encyclopedia realized that part of the story was wrong, he had doubts about the rest of the story as well. Under further questioning, Buster owned up that he had invented the whole thing. The only cousin he had lived in a skyscraper in a big city.

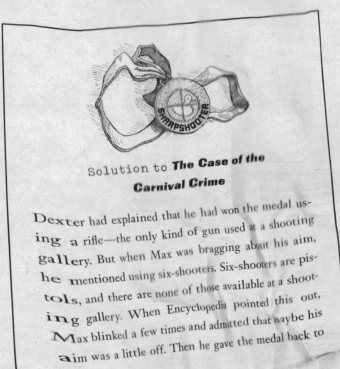

Solution to **The Case of the Carnival Crime**

Dexter had explained that he had won the medal using a rifle—the only kind of gun used at a shooting gallery. But when Max was bragging about his aim, he mentioned using six-shooters. Six-shooters are pistols, and there are none of those available at a shooting gallery. When Encyclopedia pointed this out, Max blinked a few times and admitted that maybe his aim was a little off. Then he gave the medal back to Dexter.